Camerons on the Train

Illustrated by Victor Ambrus

Macmillan & Co Ltd
London 1963

Camerons on the Train

by JANE DUNCAN

THE CHILDREN'S BOOK CLUB
121 CHARING CROSS ROAD
LONDON W.C.2.

PRINTED IN GREAT BRITAIN BY
NORTHUMBERLAND PRESS LIMITED
GATESHEAD ON TYNE

This story belongs to
SHONA, NEIL and DONALD
but
they are sharing it with their brother
IAIN
who does not come into it and cannot read as yet
but
he must not be left out.

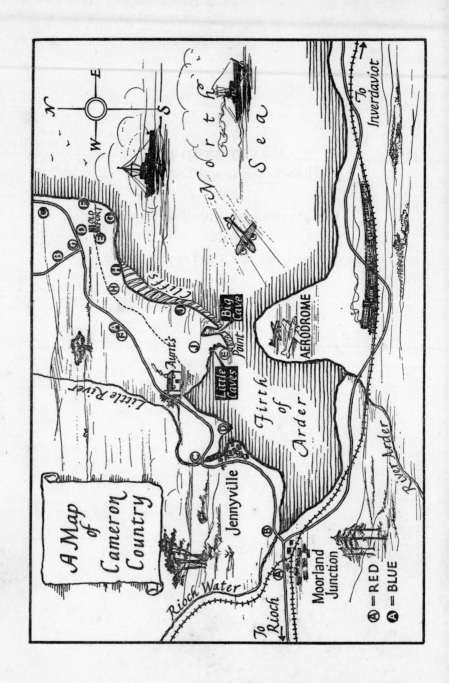

Contents

1. Lost! A Watch!

My name is Shona. I am telling you that right at the beginning because writing a story is something like speaking on the telephone and you have to tell people who you are and not be like my brother Donald, who just says: 'It's me!' Of course, he is only six. He is my second brother. Neil is my first brother. He is ten and likes to dress up and play at Cowboys and Indians and things like that. He is often very dramatic. He became very fond of being dramatic ever since Father told us a story about something that happened in the War. Father was in the Navy in this war and there was a British ship called the *Cossack* which captured a German ship called the *Altmark* that had a lot of British prisoners in it and they were all rescued, but when the British sailors knocked at the door where the prisoners were, one of them shouted out to the prisoners: 'The Navy's here!' and that, although it was only three words, made them know that they were safe and cheered them up, so it was dramatic. Ever since Father told us about this, Neil keeps charging about the garden with Donald, waving their cowboy six-shooters and shouting: 'Camerons is here!' He does this because it sounds dramatic and our name is Cameron. I have another brother called Iain, but he is only three and does not come into this story but I thought I would mention him so that he would not feel left out. I am the eldest of the family. I am thirteen.

We live near a village in Scotland called Inverdaviot, but we spend all our holidays at another village in the Highlands where our Aunt lives and last Christmas we were looking forward to going to Jennyville—that is our Aunt's village—on Boxing Day as usual when, on Christmas Eve, our brother Iain got ill. He was not very ill, but Mother said she was not going to take him out in the cold and the three of us  —Neil, Donald and I—were very disappointed until Father said: 'You three are big enough and sensible enough now to travel in the train by yourselves. I will drive you to the station and Aunt will meet you at Rioch.'

The three of us were thrilled because we do not get to travel on trains very much. Father always takes us in the car when we go anywhere. We promised to behave well and not do anything dangerous or silly and Neil said, being dramatic: 'Camerons are not silly on trains!' and Donald asked if he could have a newspaper to read on the journey. Donald is always reading. He has glasses and sometimes we call him 'The Professor' because he looks so old and wise when he is reading.

On the morning of Boxing Day, Father drove us to the station and we got on the train. It was a proper steam-engine puffing train, because they did not have the new diesel engines on the railway up where we live last Christmas. Father put us into a compartment with two ladies in it and the train started to move out at exactly nine-forty by our watches as it was supposed to do. It is only Neil and I who have watches. Donald is not big enough yet.

We sat down to read our books. Mine was called *The Helpful Giant* and very funny and Neil's was a cowboy one and, of course, Donald had his newspaper. He cannot really read properly yet, although he is always doing it, and he gets a lot of the big words wrong. I mean that he reads the loud bit of the words in the wrong place. I will put letters in italics for the loud bits to show you how he says the words.

When the train started, he first of all began to read all the things on the walls of the compartment, the names of the pictures, like: ' " York Min*ster* ' " and ' " Can*ter*bury C*ath*edral ', " and then ' " Communi*ca*tion Cord. Pen*al*ty for *im*proper use five pounds ", ' and, after that, he began to read his newspaper.

" ' Dan*ger*ous robbery at Bir*ming*ham! " ' he read

out. ' " Gang seize truckload of chemicals. Explosives also missing ".'

It all sounded so exciting that Neil and I sat down,  one on each side of him, and read about this robbery too and Neil began being dramatic and being a policeman chasing these robbers in a fast car. The two ladies got up, collected their bags and moved up the corridor to another compartment so I said to the boys: 'Look here, you two, Father said to behave ourselves and I've got a feeling we're not doing it.' Then we all looked at each other for a moment before Neil and I went back to our books and left Donald to his newspaper.

It is a very dull journey from Inverdaviot to Rioch, along the coast with nothing but sea on one side and moors on the other until you come to Arder, where the big Air Force base is. The aerodrome lies between the railway and the sea, but the railway is high up on an embankment and you can see over the high fence round the aerodrome and, if you are lucky, you might catch a whole squadron of aeroplanes on the runways.

It is at Arder that the Air Force has its big new type of aeroplane, the Jupiter, and Neil and I had heard on the wireless that if the weather stayed clear of fog they were going to be doing its test flights any day now, so we were hoping we might see it on the aerodrome when the train went past. However, although there were lots of other aeroplanes this day, Neil said that the Jupiter was not among them, so we ate the last of our chocolate, then took turns at going to the lavatory at the end of the corridor, by which time the train was coming into the outskirts of Rioch.

We got out and I could see Aunt away down at the end of the platform and I remembered that I was to ask her to telephone home to Father from the station, so I wondered if the train was on time or whether he was waiting for us to ring and wondering if we had got lost. I put down my case to look at my watch and it was not there! And then I remembered that I had taken it off in the lavatory in the train when I washed my hands and I must have forgotten to put it on again.

I just said: 'My watch!' and ran back up the platform, away up to the very end of the train where we had been and it was only when I got there that I found that Neil and Donald had dropped their bags too and were close behind me.

We got up into the corridor and ran along to the end but the door of the lavatory was shut and the little round thing said: 'Engaged', so I said we would just have to move along the corridor a bit and wait for the person to come out. We waited for quite a time but nobody came and we had just decided to go and knock on the door when the train began to move! This was very strange, for Father had said that the train did not go any further than Rioch and that we were to take our time about getting off.

'Golly! We're off!' Neil said, being dramatic.

'Where are we going?' Donald asked.

You know how it is when somebody asks you a question and you do not know the answer. I felt worried because I did not know where the train was going and there was Donald staring at me through his glasses and Neil not caring about anything but just being dramatic.

'Gosh, Neil Cameron, we'll be in proper trouble when Father finds out about this! You two shouldn't have followed me!' I said.

Neil stopped being dramatic and said: 'Father said we were to keep together all the time and go to a policeman if anything went wrong.'

'There aren't any policemen on trains, stupid!' I told him.

'Or the guard, Father said,' Donald said. 'Father said the guard.'

Neil and I looked down at him and he was looking very professorish and clever through his glasses. Sometimes I think he really *is* clever.

'That's just what I was going to say!' I said, glaring at Neil, and then: '*Policeman*, my foot! Come on!'

'Whee-ee-ee! The train's stopping!' Neil said, getting dramatic again, but it was true.

The train went more and more slowly and then stopped altogether.

'We're only in the siding,' Neil said. 'Let's get out!'

'My watch!' I said and looked at the door of the lavatory and I saw the little round thing change from 'Engaged' to 'Vacant'.

Three porters came barging out of the lavatory, charged through between us, opened the door and jumped down the long way to the ground. They knocked Donald down against the wall and he was frightened and began to cry and just then the guard came along the corridor from the other end. He asked us what we were doing here and what was the matter with Donald and Donald said: 'There's nothing the matter and I'm not crying!' So then I told the guard about coming back to get my watch, so he came into the lavatory and helped us to look for it but it just was not there. I knew exactly where I had left it but it was not anywhere in that little room. We looked everywhere, so there was nothing to do but go with the guard when he said that Aunt would be looking for us and that she would be worried.

There was no platform here in the siding, so the

guard had to lift us down and then we saw Aunt coming across the lines with another man, who was the ticket-collector, so we told them what had happened. The ticket-collector said we must report about my watch at the station office but Aunt said in a stern voice: 'The first thing we have to do is telephone Father and let him know you are in Rioch!'

We went to the telephone box and, of course, Donald started reading everything like: '"In case of emer*genc*y dial 'O' and ask for police or ambu*l*ance",' and Neil got dramatic and kept saying: 'Police here! We'll be there right away!' and nobody seemed to care about my watch.

However, when we went to the station office, the man in there was very interested and asked me to

describe my watch, so I told him that Grandpa gave it
to me for my tenth birthday, that it was gold with a
brown leather strap and on the back of the watch itself
there were my initials and Grandpa's, written like this
'SC/AE', which meant that Shona Cameron got the
watch from Adam Eddie, for that is Grandpa's name.
After that, he asked if I could remember where the
train was when I went to the lavatory but I could not
remember exactly about this until Donald said : ' It was
just after the aeroplanes ! ' So then we knew that the
train had been between Arder and Rioch, because the
aerodrome is at Arder.

When we came out of the office, though, I simply
started to cry because I could not help it. I was so sorry
about losing my watch right at the beginning of the
holidays and everything and Aunt said : ' We'll put an
advertisement in the newspaper tomorrow, Shona. We
can't do it today because the office will be closed on
Boxing Day.' After that, I felt a lot better. It seemed to
give me some hope.

The next morning, Aunt telephoned to the newspaper in Rioch and the day after that it was very exciting because in the column headed 'Lost and Found'
there was this notice :

'Lost on the morning train Inverdaviot/Rioch,
Boxing Day, gold watch engraved on back
SC/AE reward to finder Box 381.'

I gave all my holiday money to Aunt — and Neil and Donald put in half-a-crown each of theirs — to pay the reward but two days after the advertisement we had not heard anything and Aunt said: 'I'm afraid the watch is gone for good, Shona, but never mind. It was an accident — you can't be sure you left it in the lavatory.'

But I *was* sure, because I could remember taking it off and putting it down on the little shelf and then Donald said: 'I bet those porters what knocked me *down* took it!'

'Crooks!' Neil said.

'What porters, Donald?' Aunt asked.

So we told her about how they had barged out and jumped down and run away across the siding.

'It seems queer,' she said. 'But I don't think you must accuse the railway men of taking the watch, Donald.'

'*They* knocked me *down*!' Donald said.

But there was no use in arguing like that, Aunt said. It would not do any good and it would not bring back my watch.

2. Found! A Boat!

NEIL, Donald and I like to go to Aunt's because there is always lots to do, especially in the summer. We have a lot of friends there in the summer holidays —people who come to their holiday houses at Jennyville—but we are the only ones who go in the winter. All the other houses are shut up in the winter, except the post office, the police station and Aunt's, of course.

In the summer, you can fish for flounders in the Little River or collect shells on the shore or collect wild flowers on the hills at the back of the house, but we like the shore best, especially the Little Caves. We play at Pirates or Smugglers there, mostly, but this holiday I am telling you about we went down to the Little Caves on the first morning for a different reason, because the Point, where the caves are, is just across the Firth from the aerodrome at Arder and Neil said they might be going to test the Jupiter that day. It was very frosty and clear and cold but we were quite warm in tartan trousers and thick sweaters which were some of the things we got at Christmas. And the boys had their cowboy hats and two water pistols each in holster belts which were their extra presents from Aunt. Aunt sends us Christmas presents to have on Christmas Day at home and we get our extra presents when we arrive at Jennyville. My extra present was a game called

'Scrabble' for us to play in the evenings when it was
dark outside.

Down at the Little Caves, we watched the aerodrome for quite a time and although we saw lots of
aeroplanes take off and land and an Air Sea Rescue
launch roaring through the water on its practice run,
we did not see the Jupiter, so the boys put their cowboy
hats on upside-down and we played at Pirates for a
while.

When we began to feel hungry for dinner — we do
not wear our watches on the beach but our stomachs
tell us when to go home — we decided not to go home
up the beach as we had come, but to climb up the rocky
slope above the caves and go back over the fields. It was
when we were up on the fields above the Point that we
saw the boat, sailing up into the Firth from the North
Sea. If you look at the map that Father drew, you will
see what I mean.

The queer thing was that it was a boat that looked
like a yacht but it did not have its sails up. It did not
have oars either and there was no noise of an engine,
nor could we see anybody in it. It seemed to be floating
along, all by itself.

Neil said :

    ' "I bit my arm, I sucked the blood
      And cried A sail ! A sail !" '

—which is a piece of poetry and he was being

dramatic, of course, but the boat did not have any sails.

Another queer thing was that nobody sails up there in the Firth in the winter, although in summer there are lots of yachts over on the other side, near the aerodrome, and Father takes us to the regatta there in the summer holidays, but I had never seen a boat sailing in the Firth in the Christmas holidays before except for the Air Sea Rescue launches, of course, but they do not sail for fun. I said that the people in this boat must be dippy to be sailing on a cold day like this but Neil said that he wished they would take *him* for a sail, dippy or not, and we had a bit of an argument until Donald said: 'Let's wave and see if anybody pops up and waves back!' We all turned round to wave, but there was not any boat! It simply was not there. It had just disappeared. It was a very funny feeling to stand there on the Point and look down to where that boat had been and see no boat at all when we had only turned our backs for a minute or so.

'It must have sinked!' Donald said.

'Plunged headlong in the tide!' Neil said, getting dramatic again.

I did not say anything. I kept looking down at the water and the beach. The tide was coming in and it was right up to the cliffs of the Point, round on the east side where we were not allowed to go, because there was no beach there when the tide was in. Even at high tide there is always a good bit of beach on the side where the Little Caves are and, besides, Aunt can see us on that side, with her field-glasses, from the house and, if we lose our tempers and start throwing mud or anything, she rings a big brass bell she has.

I kept on staring but that boat simply was not there and I did not believe it could have sunk as Donald said because the sea was quite calm and those yachts can turn upside down and still go on floating. We saw one turn upside down at the Regatta once and the men sailing it climbed up and sat astride its keel until another boat went out to fetch them.

' It's very mysterious,' I said.

' The case of the vanishing boat ! ' Neil said. ' Listen, let's go home to dinner and then play detectives ! '

We went home, but I thought there was too much vanishing going on this holidays — first my watch and now this boat.

After dinner, we went down to the beach again and up on the Point and looked down on the other side from the Little Caves. We crawled down fairly close to the edge of the cliffs, which we were not allowed to do even although there is a fence along the top, and looked over but there was no boat down there, just the water going lap-lap-lap at the bottom of the cliffs. Then we heard the bell ringing from the house and that meant that Aunt had seen us on the wrong side of the Point through her field-glasses, so we ran back down to the Little Caves and played at Smugglers until it was dark.

The next day was Thursday 28th of December. I know the date because that was the day of the advertisement about my watch and I still have the newspaper. While Neil and I were reading the advertisement, Donald was reading the other side of the newspaper in the way he does.

' "*Sus*pected sa*bot*age attempt on Ju*pite*r!" ' he read out.

'Jupiter?' Neil said. 'Here, gimme that paper!'

There really was not much about the suspected sabotage. The paper only said that it understood that two men who had been loitering near the aerodrome had been arrested by the police and it was believed that they were suspected of being saboteurs, but there was a tremendous lot about the Jupiter itself, all things that Neil had read before and knew already but, still, he had to read them all over again. Neil simply can never get enough of something like the Jupiter.

'That old Jupiter!' I said, for I wanted to read about my watch again.

'The Jupiter is a perfect TV star of an aeroplane,' Aunt said. 'It's always in the headlines.'

Donald had now got behind the newspaper again and had found some more big print to read.

' "Scottish police *al*erted. Bir*ming*ham chem*i*cal thieves believed to have driven north." — That's the ones that were in my newspaper I had on the train,' he said. 'When will they catch them, Aunt?'

'If *I* was a policeman, *I'd* soon catch them!' Neil said. 'It's all up!' He got dramatic and forgot about the Jupiter. 'The police is here! Stick 'em up!'

When we went down to the beach that morning, we played at detectives and chemical thieves for a while, then we watched to see if they would test the Jupiter over at the aerodrome and it was then that Neil said: 'Listen, what about that boat we saw yesterday?' and I do not know quite how it happened but, quite soon, the three of us were walking round the beach to the other side of the Point where we are not allowed to go.

The tide was out and there was a little bit of beach but it was very stony and seaweedy and nasty and not a bit like our own side where the Little Caves are. In fact, it was just plain dull, with the high cliffs on one side and the water on the other side of this little beach, so we decided to turn back, but, first of all, we took a last look along the coast to see if that boat was there and it was then that Neil got all dramatic and said: 'Open Sesame! I see a cave!' and ran away from Donald and me and along the shore.

Of course, we ran after him and we came to a sort of slit in the cliffs not much wider that Aunt's garden gate and the light inside was quite dim. Donald and I did not want to go in, really, because it was all so dim

and smelly and all slippery with seaweed but Neil
said: 'I'm going in!' so we all had to go. We could
not see anything at first but after a little our eyes became
used to the dim light and we could see the green slimy
stuff hanging down from the rocks and that the
cave was much bigger inside than it looked from
outside.

'Golly, gosh and golly!' Neil said. 'The boat!'
and he pointed into the dimness and, sure enough,
there was the boat, and I was sure it was the very one
we had seen the day before.

It was sitting on the seaweedy stones and tied to an
iron ring that was fixed in the rock and had an anchor
lying beside it, attached to it with another rope. On
each side of its bows it had its name in white: *Lady
Fair*, but although it had this name it was pretty messy,
its paint all scratched and chipped. But Neil and

Donald thought it was splendid, so we played in it at being savage Vikings in our Long Ship. When we play Vikings, Neil is Neil Long-Tooth, Donald is Donald Black-Beard and I am Shona of the Long Hair.

It was while we were playing that I discovered that, at the back of the cave, the floor rose up into a sort of ledge, nearly as high as a table but not quite, so Donald and I climbed on the ledge, which made a splendid iceberg for being marooned on, and we were rescued by Neil Long-Tooth in his Long Ship. There were so many things you could do around the boat and the cave was less smelly when you were used to it that we nearly forgot about dinner-time and had to run along the shore, sneak round the Point close to the rocks and then run again up our own beach to the house.

Just at the garden gate, Neil said that we must keep the boat a secret because, if we let Aunt know about it, she would forbid us to play in it for it was somebody else's property and I said we simply *had* to keep it a secret because it was round the wrong side of the Point and Aunt would be even more forbidding about *that*. Sometimes, when Neil gets very enthusiastic and dramatic about things, he forgets all the more ordinary things, things that he knows quite well, like our not being allowed to play on the wrong side of the Point.

When we went down to the beach again after dinner, though, the tide was in and we could not get round to the boat at all, so we played at Smugglers in the Little Caves instead until it was time to go home for tea, just as it was getting dark.

After tea, Aunt had the television on to hear the news and, about half-way through, the announcer said: 'There are new developments in the Birmingham Chemical Robbery.'

'These are *my* robbers in my newspaper,' Donald said and Aunt said: 'Hush for a moment!'

Then the announcer said that the lorry with the load of chemicals that had been stolen from Birmingham had been found abandoned on a coast road in the north-east of Scotland and that all the chemicals were still in it except two small wooden boxes that contained a new kind of explosive called Porontium 106, which was very powerful and dangerous. After that, he said that there was a possibility that the lorry-load of chemicals had been stolen by mistake and that the thieves had really meant to take a lorry that was full of cigarettes and sugar and things for the Chemical Works canteen, and that when they discovered they had these boxes of Porontium 106 in the lorry, they might have dumped them off just anywhere. There was a police warning, he said, that anybody who found a box—a wooden box with P-O-R-O-N-T-I-U-M (he spelled it out) 106 and a lot of X's in red painted on it — was on no account to touch it. The finder should report it at once to the nearest police station.

'Porontium 106!' Neil said, getting very dramatic. 'Bang! Bang! Ker-woosh! Bang!'

'Porontium 106 x-x-x-x!' Donald said. 'They were *my* robbers in *my* newspaper!'

'Pity the lorry didn't blow up with them,' Neil said. 'B-b-bang! Ker-woosh! Ker-lump!'

'I think,' Aunt said, 'we'll have a quiet game of Scrabble before the roof flies off the house.' So we played two games and then it was time for bed.

3. *From the Play to the Police Station*

THE next day, we did not go to the beach at all because, in the afternoon, Aunt was taking us to Rioch to see a play called *Pirates' Gold* which was being acted by some schoolchildren and their teachers in aid of the Save the Children Fund. She wanted to do some shopping in the afternoon so we left quite early and, on the way, Aunt stopped at the Post Office, which is a little over a mile from her house, and called out to the Postmistress: 'Tell Johnnie not to bother to bring my letters today! I'll pick them up on the way back.'

The Postmistress knows us three well and she came out to the car to talk to us, so we told her that we were going to *Pirates' Gold* and she said we did not need any pirates' gold when we had Neil's golden hair in the house already and this made Neil so angry that he was not dramatic even once all the way to Rioch although it takes over an hour to get there. The Postmistress meant to be pleasant, of course, and not teasing at all but Neil does not like anybody to speak about his hair, because it is really more red than gold and he hates it. At least, at this time that the Postmistress mentioned it he was still hating it, but he does not mind it now. In fact, he is quite boastful about it.

When we got to Rioch, we had some ice-cream and

then Aunt left us in Woolworth's while she did her shopping, but Neil was still sulky after being teased about his hair and went off on his own to the other end of the store while Donald and I went to where they have the pencils and rubbers and things. I had left all my holiday money at home because I was still saving it for the reward for the person who found my watch but Aunt had given me half-a-crown so that I should not feel left out if Neil and Donald bought things, so I bought a box of crayons for a shilling. I am very fond of drawing pictures, some-times.

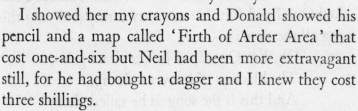

Aunt came back to Woolworth's and found us and then we went to have lunch and she said : 'What did you buy?'

I showed her my crayons and Donald showed his pencil and a map called 'Firth of Arder Area' that cost one-and-six but Neil had been more extravagant still, for he had bought a dagger and I knew they cost three shillings.

'The first little prick with that on anybody's skin,'

Aunt said, 'and I shall confiscate it, Neil Cameron. Now, you *will* be careful, won't you?'

Neil got all red in the face and promised to be careful but I think he felt that he was having an unlucky day, with the Postmistress saying things about his hair and now Aunt being stern about his dagger, so, to help him out, I said: 'What's in that other parcel, Neil?'

'None of your business!' he said snappily, which was very nasty when I was trying to be helpful but I knew that it was probably sweets. Neil never goes anywhere without spending some of his money on sweets.

After lunch, we went to the hall where the play was being given and it was all very exciting and Neil quite forgot to be sulky about his hair any more. The play was all about buried treasure — gold doubloons and pieces of eight — and the Pirate Chief was called One-Eyed Jim and wore a black patch over one eye. A boy and girl called Peter and Susan found his treasure in the cave where he had buried it and in the end One-Eyed Jim walked the plank and drowned himself in the sea to get away from the people who were trying to catch him. I was very sorry about this because I had liked One-Eyed Jim. He was very funny and sang this song all the time: —

> 'Oh, I'm One-Eyed Jim, a pirate grim,
> The blackest of knaves unhung,
> And this is the song as he sailed along
> That this one-eyed pirate sung: —

Oh, HO, I'm One-Eyed Jim a pirate grim—'
—and he just went on singing the same song until
everybody in the audience
was singing it too. At the end
of the play, when he walked
the plank over the rail of his
ship and fell into the sea at
the back of the stage with a
big splash, I felt quite sad for
a moment as the curtain
came down, but when it
went up again, there he was
in the middle of all the
players in his black hat with
the dagger stuck in it and
with the black patch over

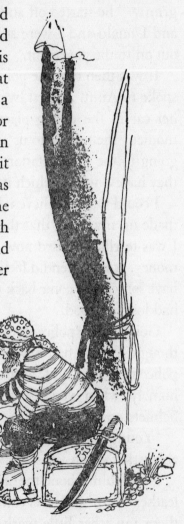

his eye, and his clothes did not even look wet. It was only then I remembered that it was all a play.

'Oh, ho, ho, HO, I'm One-Eyed Jim, a pirate grim —' he started off and we all sang again and Neil and Donald and I were still singing it when we came out on to the pavement.

It was then that the policeman stepped forward and spoke to Aunt. At first, we thought she must have left her car in the wrong place or something, but after a moment she turned to us and said: 'Children, we are going to the police station. Shona, the policeman says they have a watch which may be yours.'

I could hardly believe it! By this time, I had almost made up my mind that the watch was really gone but I was terribly pleased now that I had kept the reward money. It is a splendid feeling that I cannot describe to have something come back to you that you thought you had lost for good.

Going to the police station made us feel very solemn, though, for we had never been to one before, but the policemen look quite different and very pleasant and homely when you see them indoors without their helmets on.

'Young lady,' one of them said to me, 'tell me about this watch you lost.'

I told him about the initials on the back and the leather strap and everything and then he said: 'Is there any other little mark on it?'

'Father bored a hole!' Donald said.

'Yes!' I told the policeman. 'When Grandpa gave it to me, the strap was too long and Father bored another hole with a darn-ing needle. It isn't such a tidy hole as the other five.'

'Well, well, it's *your* watch we've got all right,' he said and, opening a drawer of his desk, he took out my watch, but he did not give it to me. He laid it on his blotter.

'I left the reward money at home, to be safe,' I said, 'but Aunt will—'

'That's all right, missy. What's your name?' he asked.

'Shona Cameron.'

'Now, Shona—' and he looked at the boys.

'And he's my brother Neil and he's my brother Donald,' I told him.

'I see. And you are staying with your Aunt for the holidays?'

'Yes.'

We looked at Aunt sitting on a chair at the end of the desk smoking a cigarette, but she just smiled and nodded at us, so we looked back at the policeman. He was a very big one, oldish, with grey hair.

'Now, Shona, I want you to tell me all you can remember about the other people you saw in the train last Tuesday. Your father put you on the train at Inverdaviot, is that right?'

'Yes.'

'Did many people get on besides yourselves?'

'A lady with a baby. It had a red coat,' I said.

'And a man with a gun and a dog,' Neil said. 'He put the dog in first and it jumped out again and then he had to lift it in again. It was a big black retriever.'

'My, you've got good memories!' he said. 'What about *you*, Donald?'

'I saw two boys — big boys — that had golf clubs and I saw the Guard waving his flag.'

'That's the lot from Inverdaviot, sir,' another policeman said.

I had not noticed him before because he was sitting at a table behind us with a lot of papers in front of him.

'Now, did you see anybody get on the train at any of the other stations?' the oldish one asked.

'No,' I told him, 'because Father said not to put our heads out of the windows.'

'And quite right too. Now, you were in a corridor carriage?'

'Yes.'

'Which one? Can you remember? Was it up near the engine or down at the end?'

'The very end,' I said.

'Was *not*, stupid!' Neil said. 'It was the one right next to the engine!'

'It was not! We had to run all the way back up the platform—'

'It was next to the engine at Inverdaviot!' Neil shouted.

'That's fine, lad,' the big policeman said. 'You're sure of that?'

'Yes, sir, dead sure!' Neil said, getting dramatic.

'And it came into Rioch station backwards, the train did,' Donald said and the big policeman said: 'That's right, son.'

'Now, did you take a walk up and down the corridor at all?' he asked.

I looked at Aunt. We had been told not to walk about the train and not to leave the compartment unless we *had* to go to the lavatory, but she just smiled and nodded again in an encouraging way.

'Quite a bit,' I said, 'but we didn't go over the shaky bit where our carriage joined the next one.'

'I see. Now, there were a lot of compartments in that carriage. Just try to imagine you are back in the train. You are walking along the corridor, looking in at the people in the compartments and the train is going clickety-clack! clickety-clack! click—'

'Whee-ee-ee! It whistled before the bridge!' Neil said.

'That's right. Now, who do you see in the compartments?'

We all began to speak at once.

'Two ladies, one had a brown coat and one a black one. They were in with us at first and then they moved.'

'Three gentlemen——'

'——and one of them was reading a magazine about aeroplanes!'

The policeman held up his hand. 'Just a minute, now——these three gentlemen——what were they like? Old like me?'

'No, sir,' Neil said. 'They were more like him,' and he pointed to the policeman at the table. 'One of them was writing in a notebook with a pen the same as Father's.'

'A Morton 83,' Aunt told the oldish policeman.

'These would be the three commercial travellers, sir,' the policeman who was sitting at the table said.

'Right, Dickson,' the old policeman said to him and looked back at us again. 'Off we go! Clickety-clack! Clickety-clack! Who else?'

'A man and a woman and a baby and a little boy,' I said.

'And three men playing cards,' Neil said.

The big policeman held up his hand again. 'Uh-huh? And what were *they* like? Old like me?'

'No, sir.'

'Like Dickson?'

'*No*, sir!'

'Well, now,' he said and he opened another drawer of his desk, 'I wonder if they were anything like any of the people in these pictures.'

He brought out a great heap of photographs of men and spread them all over his desk.

'Gosh, sir, are these all *criminals*?' Neil asked.

'No, Neil. These are what we call types. They aren't pictures of real people at all. Now, take a good look and see if you can show me one that looks anything like any of these three men you saw playing cards.'

'Now, take your time,' Aunt said. 'Take a good look before you say anything.'

But it was not very long before Donald pointed and said: 'That one, Neil. That picture is like the one that told us to clear out.'

'Yes, sir,' Neil said, 'that *is* like him.'

'So you spoke to them?' the policeman asked.

I did not know about this. The boys must have spoken to the men while I was washing my hands or something. I washed my hands two or three times on the train.

'Well, not exactly, sir. We were just watching them playing cards from outside the window — it wasn't a game that we can play — and that one — ' he pointed to the picture ' — opened the door a little bit and said: "Geedat, youse keeds!" — so we went away.'

'Is that how he said it? In a voice like that? Say it again, Neil.'

'Geedat, youse keeds!' Neil said and the policeman looked at Aunt.

'Probably fairly accurate,' she said. 'Neil is quite a mimic.' But she was smiling again so it was all right.

'Well, we're doing fine,' the policeman said. 'Now, can you remember any more? Have another look at the pictures.'

We looked carefully at them all but we did not find another one that was like the men, so they were all put back in the drawer except the one that we had picked out.

'And you can't remember one more thing about them?' the policeman asked.

It was then that I noticed Neil's face getting very red and he put his hands in his coat pockets and hunched himself up instead of standing straight, but Aunt had noticed it too and she said : 'Speak up, Neil! What is it?'

'Nothing.'

'Neil, this is very important. Are you sure there isn't anything?'

Neil looked at the big policeman, gave a big gulp in his throat and said : 'One of the men — not the one that told us to clear out — it was the one sitting opposite him —'

'Yes, Neil?'

'He had hair—hair the same colour as mine,' he said, his face going very red, and then he looked down at his toes.

'Good *lad*!' the policeman said, very pleased.

'Now, that's a real *big* help!—Well, thank you all very much. But, listen, Neil, before you go home, would you like to meet a real detective inspector from Scotland Yard? We've got one with us here at the moment.'

'Oh, *sir*!' Neil said, lifting his head and taking his hands out of his pockets.

'Then come with me, the three of you,' he said and led us through to another smaller room.

Behind the desk there was sitting a man dressed in

an ordinary suit like Father's but the queerest thing was that he had hair that was even redder than Neil's! He left the desk and shook hands with us all and then our big old policeman said: 'There were three men on that train, one of them this type—' and he gave him the picture we had chosen '—and one of them with red hair like yours and Neil's here.'

The detective inspector laughed. 'It wasn't me, was it?'

'No, sir!' Neil said indignantly. 'Nothing like you! He was a little thin man with light brown shoes!'

'Please, sir,' Donald said, looking up at this big red-haired man very solemnly through his glasses, 'there was three more men in that train—the ones in the wash-place what knocked me *down*!'

'Now, *then*,' the detective inspector said, 'just you come here and tell me all about this, report it properly. They knocked you *down*?'

So then we had to tell all about my watch and getting into the siding and everything and how the porters barged out of the lavatory, so the policeman went and fetched Aunt and she sat down beside us and started smoking another cigarette that the detective inspector gave her.

'Porters?' he said. 'They were dressed like porters?'

'Yes, with peaked caps and everything.'

'And they jumped out and ran away across the siding?'

'Yes.'

'Were they carrying anything?'

We had not noticed. It had been too quick.

'Were they big men with red hair like me?'

'Not big. They had those black caps on.'

'Was there anything funny about them?'

Neil and I looked at one another. I really had not seen them properly and I had just taken it for granted that they were porters.

'The one what knocked me *down* had beetroot under his chin,' Donald said.

'Beetroot?'

'Yes. Red like beetroot.'

The inspector opened a bottle of red ink and said to Donald: 'Take this pen and make a red blot on this blotting-paper the same size as the beetroot.'

Donald made a red blot that was sort of oval-shaped.

'It was shaped like an egg? Like that?'

'Yes.'

The detective inspector took a penknife from his pocket, cut out the blot and gave it to Donald. It was about the size of a halfpenny, but oval, as I said.

'Now, Donald, go and stick that on Inspector Wilson's chin just where it was on the man.'

'Come on, son,' our big policeman said.

'Could you put your head back a bit?' Donald asked

and he put the blot under the chin and a bit to one side. 'It was like that, only a little bit bigger and purpler,' he said.

'Donald,' Aunt said, 'was it anything like the little mark on David Murray's hand?'

'Yes. Just like that but far, far bigger.'

'A birth-mark,' Aunt said to the detective inspector and he nodded.

'Now,' he said next, 'we're going to do a bit of play-acting. Your Aunt will be Shona, Inspector Wilson will be Neil and I'll be Donald and you three will be the three men. Now, the door there is the door of the lavatory. Where were you three standing?'

We arranged ourselves as we had been in the train with me in the middle and Donald at the corner, nearest to the door.

'Right,' he said. 'Well, your Aunt, Wilson and I will stand where you are and you three go outside and come barging in when I count three. Shona, you are the biggest, so you will be the one that knocks me down. I'm Donald, remember.'

We went out and shut the door and when we heard ' one-two-three! ' we came plunging in, just as the men had done and I knocked sidewise against the detective inspector and he fell down just like Donald. Then a queer thing happened. Neil jumped right over the big man lying on the floor and as he jumped he said : ' Demn dese keeds! '

The detective inspector sat up and looked at us. ' That's what happened? ' he asked. ' A man jumped over Donald and said —'

' DEMN DESE KEEDS! ' Neil said again and then became very dramatic. ' These porters weren't porters at all! They —'

' No! ' I said, interrupting him. ' They were the men that —'

' — were playing cards —'

' — and chased Neil and me away! ' Donald ended.

The big red-haired man, still sitting on the floor and looking very funny, began to laugh.

' You are quite sure you all remember the man saying that when he jumped over Donald? Are you sure, Shona? '

' Yes, quite sure. I didn't remember about it until Neil said it, though.'

' I didn't remember it myself, sir, until I was jumping over you and then it just came out.'

'It was the one with the beetroot on him what said it,' Donald said. 'I don't like *him*.'

'I should think not!' the detective inspector said. 'Well, that's splendid and we'll let you go home now but we may come to see you people again and if you think of anything more, ask your Aunt to telephone us. And now, thank you very much.'

It was all so exciting that I can hardly remember any more of that night, but I know that we had to have supper in town before we went home because we were so hungry. And another thing was that I did not get my watch back, but that was all right, because the policeman said they would keep it safely and that I would get it back in the end.

4. *Marooned in the Cave*

THE next morning, it was too wet even for us to go out-of-doors, although Aunt says that we turn into duck-fish when we come to Jennyville, but she also said: 'Rain before seven, sun before eleven' and that it might be a fine afternoon although perhaps not very sunny, being nearly the end of December. We did not mind staying in, really, because we had so much to talk about and Aunt said we had 'behaved very well' at the police station the day before, a thing that she had never said to us before in our lives.

We asked her how the police knew we were at *Pirate's Gold* and she told us that they had been down here at Jennyville looking for us and the Postmistress had told them where we were.

Then I remembered that we had not asked the police for the name and address of the person who had found my watch so that we could send the reward money, but Aunt said we would not have to pay a reward now because it was the police who found the watch, but she thought it would be a good idea to give the reward to the Save the Children Fund instead and that is what we decided to do.

'But *how* did the police find it?' Neil asked.

'It was a lucky accident, really,' Aunt said. 'I rang up the police about the watch the same day that we put the advertisement in the newspaper and it so happened they were investigating a burglary that day. There is a shop in Rioch that buys and sells second-hand clothes and furniture and jewellery and things and the police suspect that this shopkeeper sometimes buys things from thieves. They went to search his shop for some jewellery that had been stolen in the burglary but they didn't find it. They found Shona's watch instead.'

'I bet it was those three men on the train that took it and sold it to this man!' Neil said.

'Yes. I think that's what the police think too,' Aunt agreed and then she said to me: 'So your watch isn't a watch at the moment, Shona. It's a *clue*!'

'Geedat youse keeds!' Neil said in his mimicking voice. 'That's a clue, too, isn't it?'

'Yes.'

'And my beetroot is a clue?' Donald asked.

'Yes, that's a *very* good one, Donald. It was very clever of you to see that mark. How did you?'

'Well, you see, they knocked me *down*! And I was lying on the floor of the train like this'—Donald lay down on the floor—'and he jumped over me—'

'Like this!' Neil said, going dramatic and jumping over Donald. 'Demn dese keeds!'

'Yes and so I was looking up at him from right underneath and I saw it,' Donald said.

'Well, it's a splendid clue,' Aunt told him.

'And the picture we picked out is another clue?' I asked.

'Oh, yes. You found lots of them. Neil's one about the little man with red hair and brown shoes was a good one too.'

'Not very good, really,' Neil said. 'He'll probably dye his hair if he knows the police are after him.'

'Maybe,' Aunt said. 'Well, I must go and see about the dinner. It's still raining awfully hard but I do believe it will clear up in the afternoon.'

Aunt went off to the kitchen and we sat around the fire and talked a bit more about all the clues we had found until Donald said: 'I wish we had some sweets for a wet day'—and that made us all think of sweets. We had meant to buy sweets to bring home after we had been to the play the day before but, of course, with all the business of going to the police station we forgot and all the shops were shut anyhow. Then I remembered about the parcel that Neil had been rude to me about at lunch the day before, so I said: 'Neil, you bought sweets yesterday!'

'No, I didn't,' he said.

'Neil Cameron, that's a great big fib! You had a parcel that was a jar of boiled sweets!'

'It was *not* sweets!'

'Then, what was it?'

'None of your business!'

'You're very rude! And I don't believe you! You've got sweets and you're just being mean! Selfish greedy-guts!'

'Yes, greedy-guts!' Donald said.

Neil's face got very red. 'Honestly, Shona—one Cameron to another—it wasn't sweets,' he said.

'What was it then?'

'You won't tell?'

'Of course not!' I said.

'Acourse not!' Donald said.

'All right. Come upstairs and I'll show you.'

We went up to the boys' bedroom and Neil took the parcel out of his secret hole behind the books on the bookshelf.

'I haven't even opened it,' he said, 'because it was just a waste of money after all. A whole half-crown, it cost. Here, you open it, Shona.'

I opened the parcel. Inside was a packet with a bottle in it and when I took the bottle out and read the label, it said: 'Draper's Dependable Dye. Jet Black.'

'What in the world did you buy this for?' I asked and his face got terribly red.

'I was going to dye my hair,' he mumbled, not being in the least dramatic.

'Oh Neil *Cameron*!' I said and my legs felt so wobbly that I had to sit down on the bed.

Donald sat down beside me and we both simply stared at Neil for we were both completely astounded, and this seemed to make him feel better. He puffed out his chest and strode across the floor with his thumbs in his belt like One-Eyed Jim in the play.

'But it was just a waste of half-a-crown,' he said in a grand way, 'because I'm going to keep my hair the way it is now. *I* don't mind about it being red. When I'm big, I'm going to be a detective inspector at Scotland Yard. I've got the right colour of hair for it!'

Then he got very dramatic, picked up an imaginary telephone and said: 'Dickson, come in here for a moment, will you?' and his voice was just like the voice of the detective inspector at Rioch. Neil really *can* mimic people awfully well.

'Pity I wasted that half-crown, though,' he said next, turning into himself again.

'We could use the dye for ink, maybe,' Donald suggested.

We all thought about it for quite a bit, because we are always worried if we waste any of our money. There are always so many things that we want that we never have enough money to buy and here we were with a whole half-crown's-worth of black dye that we did not want at all.

'We'll keep it anyhow,' I said in the end. 'Aunt says that if you keep a thing for seven years it's bound to come in useful, but you'd better hide it again or we won't get a chance to keep it for even seven minutes.'

When we went downstairs, the postman had been and had brought the newspapers, so, of course, Donald took the local one which is printed in Rioch and began to read : ' " Porontium 106 still unfound. Thieves still at large. Police have new in*form*ation. From new e*vid*ence obtained, the Rioch police have issued a request for in*form*ation about three men who are required for qu-questioning. It is believed that the men are of slim build, of medium height or less, that one has ow-au*burn* hair and a second has a red birth-mark on the neck under the left jaw and speaks with a foreign accent. Anyone with in*form*ation of men of this *des*cription—" '

' Golly ! ' Neil said, being very dramatic, ' That's us Camerons' three men ! Well, just think ! We could have caught them at the station that day ! We could have got a rope and tied the door of the wash-place to the door of the corridor and —'

' Be quiet ! ' I said. ' I'm reading ! '

The newspaper went on to tell all over again about how the lorry with the chemicals had been stolen and then it said that the police were watching the ports all over Scotland because the men might be trying to escape by sea.

We talked about it all through dinner but when we were helping Aunt with the washing-up afterwards we noticed that the rain had gone off and after she had had a look out of the back door at the hills, Aunt said it was really going to clear up and that we could go out.

We got into our Wellington boots and wind-breakers and the boys got their cowboy hats and water pistols and Neil's new dagger and his torch and we went off down to the Little Caves. The tide was quite a bit out so we walked down to the edge of the water to look across at the aerodrome to see if the Jupiter was out on the runway, but it was not, so we came back to the Point.

'Let's go round to the boat!' Neil said.

This made us all look up at the house, thinking of Aunt and her field-glasses.

'She'll be reading,' Neil said in a low voice. 'She reads even more than Donald.'

We looked up at the house again and then began to tiptoe round the Point, which was silly, when I thought about it, but yet you always feel you have to speak in whispers and tiptoe if you are doing some-thing secret, even if nobody is there to hear you.

Once we were round the Point, though, we stopped tiptoeing and began to run along the stones. On this side of the Point, the water does not go away far out as it does on our own side because it is a much steeper beach, so there is just a narrow stony path between the water and the rocks.

With Neil's torch, we had a good look round the cave but there was nothing to be seen except the ledge and the boat and we did not use the torch much, because it only showed up all the slimy seaweed hang-

ing on the walls. We played at pirates, with Neil being
One-Eyed Jim first and then Donald and I having a
turn and we tried to open a locked-up place in the stern
of the boat, but we gave up because we felt it would be
wrong to break the lock when we were borrowing the
boat like this, so we sat down on the ledge to eat our
chocolate biscuits that Aunt had given us and played
at being shipwrecked on a raft and eating the very last
of our food. We often play at this when we have
chocolate biscuits because it makes them last a long
time.

When we had eaten the last of our food like this, we
decided that we would build one last signal fire, in the
forlorn hope that some ship would see us before we
died of starvation, so we picked all the seaweed off the

wall above the ledge at the back of the cave and piled it up like a bonfire. This had been Neil's idea but I suddenly said : 'We're on a *raft*, noodle-head! You can't have fires on rafts!'

'Never mind,' Neil said, 'the ledge is an island now.' Neil is never at a loss. Then he said sadly and in a very dramatic voice: 'This little fire is our last chance. If this fails, all is over!'

It was my turn to come to the rescue so, when Neil said this, I jumped off the ledge to go and get into the boat. When I turned round to jump, I suddenly saw that the boat was *afloat* and that the cave was full of water nearly up to the top of the ledge, but I did not quite see the water in time. I jumped and went right down nearly to my waist. It was icy cold.

At the big splash I made, Donald and Neil began to laugh at me, thinking it was a big joke, but the water was so cold that I found myself starting to cry.

'Neil Cameron!' I said, 'help me out! You too, Donald!'

The boat had floated in close to the ledge now and they jumped into it and stopped laughing. They reached over and caught my arms. I held on with my hands to the side of the boat and tried to pull myself up but my Wellington boots were full of water and heavy as lumps of lead and the water was creeping up higher and higher all around me and starting to flow over the ledge now, too.

'It's my boots!' I said. 'I'll have to get them off!'

It was a terrible struggle to get the boots off with only one hand for I needed the other one to hold on to the boat. I was afraid to let go. I can swim and have got my Girl Guide badge, but I have never swum in December, in a darkish cave with all my clothes on. At last, I got the boots off and threw them into the boat and then, with the boys pulling as hard as they could, I struggled up and fell in head-first on to the deck boards.

'Oh, Shona!' Donald said, looking worried through his glasses.

'Shona,' Neil said, 'we can't get out of here! What are we going to do?'

'I dud-dud-don't kn-know!' I said, my teeth chattering.

My legs seemed to be frozen inside my wet socks and tartan trousers and the water was running out of me into a little pool in the bottom of the boat.

'I'm so c-c-c-cold I -c-c-can't think,' I said.

It was getting quite dark now and the cave seemed different. I had never liked it very much really, with all its smelly seaweed hanging down but I was liking it less now for, the higher the boat floated, the wider the cave seemed to get and the walls went further and further away. It was horrid, sitting there in that little boat in the middle of all that dark water, for that was another thing. The cave seemed to get bigger and bigger and the water was getting deeper and deeper but the boat, which had seemed so large when we were playing around it while it was on the floor of the cave, now seemed to be terribly small and frail as it swung about on the rising tide.

'Shona,' Neil said again, 'what are we going to do?'

'I'm so c-c-c-cold,' I said.

Neil unzipped his wind-breaker. 'Take your wet socks and trousers off,' he said, 'and have this. I don't need it. I've got my big seaman's jersey on. Put your legs down the sleeves like dressing-upside-down.'

Dressing-upside-down is a game we played sometimes, just as we played at being marooned on desert islands, but I did not feel that I was playing a game when I took off my trousers and socks and put on Neil's wind-breaker upside-down.

'Do you think you can think now, Shona?' he asked.

'I'm getting awful hungry, Shona,' Donald said, 'and it's getting awful dark.'

I looked out of the mouth of the cave and away over the black water of the Firth to the aerodrome, where all the lights were on now so that it looked like a huge city, where everybody was warm and safe.

'*I* know!' Neil said. 'I'll cut the rope with my dagger and we'll float out! The opening of the cave is wider up here. Hold the torch for me, Donald!'

He took out his dagger and began to saw at the rope

that was attached to the ring on the rock but the ring was away down under the water now, of course, and I looked across at the aerodrome and thought of all these Air Force men having supper in those big warm buildings with the bright lights. Then, somehow, I thought of what Neil was doing—cutting that rope —and it came to me in a flash.

'No, Neil!' I said. 'Stop! Don't cut it!'

'Why not?' he asked.

'The tide will keep us here until it starts to ebb— we've got no oars or anything—but if we cut the ropes the tide will carry us out to sea when it turns! The deep channel is quite close to the cliffs on this side of the Point! That's why Aunt made a rule about not coming round this side!'

'Oh, oh, gosh,' Neil said, 'but it's all right, Shona. The dagger isn't very sharp and it's not cut much. But, Shona, what are we going to *do*?'

'I'm getting just awful hungry now, Shona,' Donald said, 'and it's getting darker and darker.'

'I think we'll just have to sit here,' I said, 'until the tide goes down again and we go down along with it.'

'But Shona! That'll be six whole hours and more, for it's not full tide yet!'

'I'm hungry and it's awful dark!' Donald said and started to cry.

'We must shout or *some*thing!' Neil said. 'We can't sit here and do nothing!'

We began to shout: 'Help! Help!'

5. The Royal Air Force
to the Rescue

WE shouted and shouted, but it was no use. All the shouts just went over the dark water where there was nobody to hear.

Donald, although he is only six, tries very hard to be a big boy and does not like to be treated like a baby, but he was very glad to sit on my knee now and it was warmer and safer, somehow, with him hugged close to me. Neil sat very close to me too and there we were, getting colder and colder and hungrier and hungrier, staring out across the black water at the lights of the aerodrome.

'When we play at being on a desert island,' I said, 'what do we do to get rescued?'

I was only talking because it was so creepy sitting there in the dark with no sound except the water going lick-lick-lick against the boat and the rocks.

'We wave flags at the ships that pass, Shona,' Donald said, still sobbing a little, 'and we build signal bonfires.'

'Morse!' Neil said and jumped up so suddenly that the whole boat rocked and he plumped back down on the seat again. 'Father was just starting to teach me Morse! SOS! Oh, I wish I could remember!'

'Oh, Neil! It's in my Guide Diary! SOS is three dots, three dashes and three dots! But how can you send it? We've got no wireless!'

66

'With my torch!' he said. 'Three short flashes, then three longish ones and then three short ones. Like this!' and he switched his torch off and on 'F-f-flash! Long-long-flash! F-f-flash!' up into our faces.

'Porontium 106 X-x-x-x!' Donald said and I felt like bursting out with something silly like that myself but I said instead:

'Don't waste the battery, Neil!'

'Come on up to the other end of the boat,' Neil said, 'and we'll do it across to the aerodrome! The airmen will know what it means if they see it!'

'Of *course* they'll see it!' I said.

'Acourse they will!' Donald said.

We moved up to the other end of the boat and Neil took the first turn with the torch, then we gave Donald a turn to make him forget how hungry he was and then I had a turn. It was fun at first, but it was remarkable how quickly my hands became tired, just holding the torch and pressing the button. We went on and on doing it, though, for what seemed like hours and I could see the flash growing weaker, which meant that the batteries were running down, but I did not say anything. All the same, I felt that Neil also was thinking about the batteries, although he did not say anything either. Donald began to get sleepy now and no longer wanted a turn of the torch, so I took him on my lap again and Neil went on doing the flashing.

Donald fell asleep and was very heavy, so that

between the weight of him and the cold, I felt as if I were paralysed and the flashes from the torch were growing weaker and weaker, not lighting up the cave at all now, as they had been doing at first, when Neil suddenly gave a shout that woke Donald and nearly startled me out of my wits.

'Shona! *Look*!'

Across at the aerodrome, a new lot of lights had come on down close to the water, so that we could see them reflected in it and, as we stared, we suddenly heard a deep, steady roar, like the noise of an aeroplane, but it was not an aeroplane. Lights began to move across the water.

'It's a boat! They're coming to us!' I said.

'Gosh!' Neil said. 'Oh, gosh, d'you know what? It's the Air Sea Rescue launch that rescues the airmen!'

We could see it quite clearly now, a slim grey shape with twinkling lights, cutting through the water and throwing off huge waves from each side of its bows and churning up a big wake behind it. I thought it was the most beautiful thing I had ever seen, not because I had never seen an Air Sea Rescue launch with its lights on before, which was a beautiful sight in itself, but because it was coming to help *us*.

When it was across near the Point, it slowed down, its engines died down to a purring noise as if it were a huge cat and suddenly it turned on a searchlight that went sweeping over the water and then came right over us in the cave with a beam that made us feel blind for a moment. It swept past along the cliffs and then came back again and settled on us, lighting up the whole cave for a moment, and then it tilted its beam upwards.

'Porontium 106 — x-x-x-x!' Donald said and I felt so glad to see that boat that I just had to be dramatic too.

'Yes, Donald!' I said. 'Porontium 106 — x-x-x-x!'

'It's us Camerons here!' Neil shouted, and then we heard a deep voice calling:

'Don't look into the searchlight! Turn your backs!'

We turned round and looked into the cave although we were longing to keep looking at the launch, and, behind us, we could hear it coming nearer and nearer and then we heard a voice say: 'Holy smoke, Joe! It's three kids!'

The launch came still nearer, the big light went away now right out of the cave and then a voice called: 'Okay, you can turn round now!'

We turned round. The launch was lying quite a bit out, where the water was deep, and it had its searchlight turned downwards on to the water and out of our eyes, but it had all its other lights on and it was beautiful. Up on the deck part above the bows, an officer was standing, and we could see the Air Force red, white and blue roundels and everything, and over the lighted

water two men in a small boat were rowing towards us.

'What happened?' they asked when they came near enough.

'We were playing in our boat, sir,' Neil said, 'and the tide cut us off—and we won't half catch it from Aunt when we get home!' he ended.

'Thank you very much for coming for us—' I said, '—even if we *do* catch it from Aunt,' Donald added.

None of us had really remembered about Aunt until now but the thought of her was spoiling things now, rather.

'You betcha you're going to catch it,' the airman said. 'Okay, the girl first!'

He reached out while the other man held the two boats together and lifted me out of our boat into his, then he lifted Donald and then Neil.

'Where do you live?' he asked then.

'At the house just round the Point,' I said.

'Oh, well, that's easy. Get rowin', chum!' he said to the other airman.

Then, as we passed by the launch, he shouted: 'Just goin' round to the beach round the Point here, sir!'

'All right!' a voice shouted back and then the searchlight swung round and lit up the water all round us and, when we were round the Point, it lit up the beach and there was Aunt, our village policeman and several other people. Aunt looked terribly tall and dark and stern, standing there in the white light from the launch.

'Shona,' Neil whispered, 'we should have said we lived down in London. We'd have got a sail in the launch

and we—we—well, we wouldn't have had to—to explain to Aunt!'

As a matter of fact, Aunt did not say very much or ask us to explain just then, probably because of the policeman and the postman and all the shepherds and gamekeepers from up the hill who were there and had been out looking for us. She just thanked the airman very much when we climbed out on to the beach, thanked all the other people for all the trouble they had taken and then said: 'Get along up to the house, you three!'

Neil and Donald started to run but I could not run in Neil's upside-down wind-breaker, so they slowed down and waited for me. When we were in the house, still nobody said very much, because we three were too scared to speak and Aunt did not seem to feel like being explained to, so we had baths and supper and I was quite glad to go to bed without playing Scrabble or anything, although it was only a little after eight o'clock.

I could hardly believe that it was not later than that and, when I woke up the next morning, I still could not believe it, so I went through to the boys' room and got into Donald's bed with him, just to make sure that I had not dreamed the whole thing and that I was not still dreaming. It seemed to me that we had been sitting in that boat in that dark, dreadful cave for *twelve* hours at the very least, before that beautiful launch came roaring over the dark water. It was a lovely thing to remember, though.

The boys were both awake and had their lights on when I went into the room, although it was still dark outside, and Neil was remembering too, for the first thing he said was: 'Burr-urr-urr! Gosh, remember it coming roaring across?'

'Porontium 106 — x-x-x-x!' Donald said.

We talked about the launch and being rescued for a while and then I said: 'Look here, you two, what about Aunt?'

'I know,' Neil said and he and Donald looked very solemn.

'I don't suppose it's any use apologising?' Neil asked.

Neil hates to have to apologise for anything and that even apologising was no use made him sound very hopeless.

'She maybe will never have us back to stay here again,' I said feeling very hopeless too.

'Oh, *Shona*!' Donald said. 'Shona, we'll never go round the Point no more!'

'Not even if the boat *is* there!' Neil said very dramatically. 'I swear it! As one Cameron to another!'

'That doesn't help about Aunt,' I told him and then I had an idea. 'Listen! She loves early morning tea in bed! When she stays with us, Mother always gives it to her for a treat because she has to make her own tea all the time when she is here alone.'

'Gosh, what a *brain*!' Neil said and jumped out of bed into his slippers.

'Quiet, now,' I said and we tiptoed past Aunt's door and downstairs to the kitchen.

I made the tea while the boys made some toast under the grill of the electric cooker; we laid the tray with butter and marmalade and everything and then, Neil carrying the teapot, I carrying the tray and Donald opening the doors for us, we went up to Aunt's room. We knocked and she called to us to come in.

'My goodness!' she said, sitting up in bed when she saw us with the tray and things. 'This *is* a surprise! Good morning.'

We said good morning and I gave her the tray and Neil put the teapot on it and then we just stood there until I said: 'Aunt, we're terribly sorry about last night.'

She poured herself out a cup of tea. 'Weren't you all dreadfully frightened?' she asked.

'It was *awful*, Aunt!' I said.

'And I was hungry and it was dark!' Donald said.

Neil's face got very red. 'I was scared *blue* in the face, Aunt!' he said, which was even more than apologising, for Neil hates to admit that he is ever scared of anything.

'Well, I'm not going to make a fuss,' she said. 'I

have a bit of a headache this morning, anyway, but this tea will make it better.'

'You take an aspirin and stay in bed, Aunt,' I told her. 'We'll make the dinner. I can make rice pudding—'

'—and bully beef!' This was Neil.

'And potatoes!' This was Donald.

'But what about breakfast?' she asked.

'Boiled eggs!' Neil said. 'Put them in cold water and when they start to boil, wait for three minutes.'

'Splendid,' she said. 'You go and have boiled eggs and toast and milk and we'll think about the dinner later on—But, wait a minute.'

She put down her teacup and looked at the three of us.

'You must promise me that you will *never* go round the Point again all by yourselves.'

And so we all promised.

'All right, we'll say no more about that part of it. Tell me, though, what boat was this that the airmen found you in?'

'It's a rotten old boat, Aunt!' Neil said. 'We're never going to play in it again as long as we live!'

'The Miller boys had an old boat last summer,' she said, 'but I didn't know they had left it round there. Anyway, it doesn't matter, as long as you don't go round there again. Run and have breakfast now.'

'Gosh, she was nice about it, Shona,' Neil said when we were in the kitchen.

'Yes, she *was*,' I said, 'and *I'll* tell you what, you two. We are not going down on that beach at *all* today because Aunt didn't scold us so we've got to scold ourselves.'

'Not even to the Little Caves, Shona?' Neil asked.

'Not even to the Little Caves! Get on, you, and boil those eggs.'

It was Sunday and Sundays have a way of feeling longer than any other days, especially at Aunt's, where we three do not have Sunday School to go to as we do at home. Sundays at Aunt's are usually splendid days, though, especially in the summer when we are on the beach all day, but this one was not splendid and it was terribly long.

After we had had breakfast, we got dressed and I had to wear a skirt because I had left my new tartan trousers in that rotten old boat, and skirts are a bore for playing in, but after we had dressed, Neil said: 'Shona, could Donald and I light the sitting-room fire for Aunt? I can do it. We learned about lighting fires at the Wolf Cubs.'

'Well, you'd better not make a mess on the carpet,' I told him.

'We'll put newspapers on the floor under the ash bucket just like Aunt does,' Donald said.

'And then *you'll* read the newspaper, lazybones!' Neil said.

Donald went off to the kitchen cupboard where the old newspapers are kept.

I washed up the dishes and the boys cleared out the ashes and made quite a good job of laying the fire with the small coal on top and the wood built up criss-cross underneath so that it would catch easily and we had just about finished wiping up the tiles of the hearth with a damp cloth when Aunt came downstairs.

'My goodness!' she said. 'This is wonderful! It's like having a housekeeper and two butlers!'

'Could I get to light the fire, Aunt?' Donald asked.

'Well, it's Neil's fire, really. Will you let Donald light it, Neil?'

'Oh, sure!' Neil said in a grand way. '*I* don't mind!' although I knew that he had been looking forward to lighting that fire himself.

'It's a lovely morning,' Aunt said when the fire had started to blaze. 'It's cold, but lovely sun. You'd better get off down to the beach.'

'We're not going to the beach today,' I told her.

'Not? Why not?'

'Just because.'

'Oh, all right. But I do think you should go out. It's too fine a day to fug around the house.'

'Let's go to the Old Fort, Shona!' Neil said, so we put on our wind-breakers and went off.

The Old Fort is not nearly so exciting as it sounds because it is only a round, sort of low tower without any roof. To get to it you go by a path north-east over the hill behind Aunt's (see map) and when you get there, there is nothing to do and nothing to see except miles and miles of the North Sea. In summer, it is not so bad, because there are wild flowers, and in the Easter holidays you might find a bird's nest or two in the gorse bushes that are dotted all about, but in December there is nothing to do at all.

At one time, Neil and I used to go there quite a lot, when Donald was the baby of the family, hoping that we might see a ship going past out at sea, for Neil is very interested in ships, but we never saw anything except once and then it was only a little fishing boat.

'I didn't mean to scold ourselves as much as this,' I said to Neil when we were outside and going up the hill, but Neil and Donald had turned into soldiers of the time of the Battle of Waterloo now, because people said that the Old Fort was built when it was expected that Napoleon would try to invade the country, and they took no notice of me. In between being a Waterloo soldier, Neil was being dramatic, of course, and reciting :

'"They buried him darkly at dead of night,
The sods with their bayonets turning—"'

—and the wind was very cold up here and I wished I was at home at the fire with a book. I sort of felt that things had been dramatic enough this holidays already.

When we got to the Old Fort, I did not go in through the hole in the wall but waited for the boys to finish exploring and come home again, but just after they went in I heard Donald say : 'Porontium—x-x-x-x!' and then Neil shouted to me to come and see something.

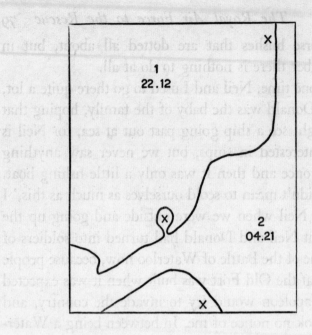

When I climbed in, it was not anything except a lot of squiggles and a few crosses and a few figures in white paint on a flat stone like this diagram that Father drew, so I said to Neil: 'Somebody's been doodling with white paint.'

'Two-nothing-four-dot-two-one,' Donald said, starting to read it all aloud. 'Is it Morse, Neil?'

'Oh dot and carry one! It *isn't* Morse!' I said. 'Come on, let's go home!'

It was colder than ever in the afternoon, so we did not go out at all. We lay on the floor and read and Donald looked at his map which he had bought in Rioch for one-and-sixpence and then all three of us studied the map and measured how far it was from Jennyville to Rioch and things like that.

When we were going to bed — we were going early and Aunt said we could read for a while before lights-out — Donald asked for a newspaper, of course, and Aunt reached out to the magazine rack and took out a paper. Then she glanced at it and said : 'Wait a minute! That's an old paper, surely? I read that bit about that stolen yacht days ago. The *Lady Fair*, it's called. I thought it a pretty name for a yacht at the time I read it.'

'Aunt — ' Neil and I said both at once.

'Yes, it's last Wednesday's paper. Oh, yes, you had it when you were lighting the fire this morning. You might as well have an up-to-date paper, Donald.'

'Aunt — ' we said again.

'Iphm? Here you are, Donald. This is yesterday's *Scotsman*. Yes, Shona?'

'Aunt — it's the boat — '

' — the boat in the cave — ' Neil said.

' — it's got *Lady Fair* written on it.'

'What?' She stared at us.

'It *has*, Aunt.'

'Sure as anything,' Donald said.

'Gracious!' she said. 'You children will drive me dotty! Are you *sure*?'

'Certain. Aunt, sorry to be a nuisance,' I said.

'Oh, Shona, I didn't really mean it! But I suppose

I'd better ring up the police. You're really quite sure?'

'Absolutely dead spifflicating certain!' Neil said, going dramatic.

'Porontium 106 — x-x-x-x!' Donald said.

Aunt got up and threw the newspaper she had been reading on top of Donald's map, which was still lying on the floor, part of it under the edge of the hearthrug, and went to the table near the window where her telephone sits.

'May I speak to either Inspector Wilson or Constable Dickson, or the detective inspector from Scotland Yard?' she asked after she had dialled. 'My name is Miss Cameron.'

'Are you getting the detective inspector?' Neil whispered to her after a moment and she nodded.

'Oh, Inspector, you remember the three children and me? Well, they've done it again. They've found this stolen yacht called the *Lady Fair*. I rang Rioch and asked for you instead of calling our local man because I thought you might believe me!' she said and laughed.

The telephone made a crackly noise that was the inspector talking back.

'In a cave about half a mile or so from the house here. No, I haven't seen it, but I don't think there's any doubt.'

I was listening and staring down at the map on the floor at the same time and thinking about the cave and the boat and everything all at once. The map was partly folded and nearly all covered up with newspaper and hearthrug except for the bit that showed the coast round about Jennyville and I got a queer kind of feeling that I had seen the map partly covered up like that before.

'Certainly, come down yourself if you think it worth while,' Aunt was saying, 'but I don't think they've remembered anything more about the other business. All right. Tomorrow morning, Inspector. We'll be delighted to see you — especially your friend Neil. Goodbye.'

She put the telephone down and said: 'Your friend is coming down in the morning. Golly, if this is a fairy-tale about this boat you *will* be in trouble — trouble with the *police*!'

'It isn't a fairy-tale, Aunt. It's —'

'Here, you two!' I said. 'Look at this!'

I took Aunt's crossword-puzzle pencil and drew lines on the map where the newspaper and the hearthrug lay on it and then put the crosses and the figures inside the lines as they had been on the stone at the Old Fort.

'Have you ever seen anything like that before?'

'The Old Fort!' Neil said.

'Porontium — x-x-x-x!' Donald said.

'What is this *now*?' Aunt asked.

We told her about the white squiggles and things on

the stone and she said : 'I can't bear any more of your mysteries tonight! Tell your inspector friend about it in the morning. It was probably drawn by some hikers in the summer. But mysteries are the inspector's business, not mine. Come along, up to bed!'

I could hardly go to sleep because of looking forward to the next day.

6. Happy New Year!

WHEN we got up the next morning, we all said: 'Happy New Year!' to one another and then made tea for Aunt as we had done the day before and went up with it and wished her a happy New Year too.

'And the same to you three!' she said. 'You know, I've been awake for quite a time but I just lay still and hoped that somebody would bring me tea and they did!'

We got dressed and Aunt made breakfast and then we helped to get all the jobs done before the inspector came. He did not arrive until eleven o'clock, but he had Inspector Wilson and Constable Dickson with him, which was splendid. They were not wearing their uniforms today and looked quite different.

We all said: 'Happy New Year!' and then Aunt said: 'Oh, dear! I forgot about the tide!' and went to the window.

'It's all right, Aunt,' Neil said. 'It started to go out about ten o' clock.'

'Yes, but we can't get round the Point yet,' Aunt said. 'I'm sorry, gentlemen, but you'll have to wait a little. I haven't got a boat.'

'We're not really on duty today,' the detective inspector said. 'This is just a little busman's holiday we three are having.'

'Then let's all have a cup of coffee,' she said.

While she went to get the coffee, we told the policemen about going to the Old Fort and the stone with
the squiggles on it and then we showed them the map.

'Isn't it mysterious, sir?' Neil asked.

The detective inspector read out the figures: 'One,
two, two, one, two. I think your aunt is right, Neil. I
think it was a rendezvous of some kind for some
hikers or maybe Boy Scouts.'

'What's a rendez-what-you said, please?' Donald
asked.

After they had all had coffee and we three had had
chocolate biscuits, Aunt said she thought we could try
to go round the Point now, so we all set off, the three
of us in front and Aunt behind with the three policemen and I could hear her telling them about the Air Sea
Rescue men rescuing us on Saturday night.

'I was nearly out of my mind,' she said, 'and I
haven't *yet* summoned up the courage to tell their
parents about it.'

'It's a wonder the newspapers haven't told them *for*
you,' Inspector Wilson said. 'The papers can be a
nuisance sometimes.'

'Oh, we're right out of the world here, you know,'
Aunt said. 'All sorts of things could happen and the
rest of the world would never know. And the few
people who live here are used to these Air Sea Rescue
launches tearing up and down at all times of the day
and night, carrying out practice runs and so on.'

When we were at the Point, we still had to wait for quite a time for the water to go back far enough to let us walk along under the cliffs to the cave, and Neil whispered to me: 'Shona, what if the boat's gone?'

'Gone? It can't be *gone*!' I said.

'Well, it *came* in a queer way. It could go just as queerly.'

'Oh, Neil! If it's gone, Aunt *will* send us home in disgrace!'

'Oh, *Shona*!' Donald said.

All three of us held our breath practically all the way along to the cave, but the boat was still there, lying on the wet stones. Neil and I gave long sighs of relief but Donald jumped up and down and said: 'Porontium — x-x-x-x!'

'What's that?' the detective inspector said, looking seriously at Donald.

'Oh, he's always saying that, sir, since he read about the robbery; silly little chump!'

Neil was being very dramatic and grown-up with the red-haired detective, especially now that the old boat was there after all.

'Am *not* a silly chump!' Donald said. 'It's up there on the wall!'

'*What* is, Donald?' Aunt asked.

'Porontium — x-x-x-x!' Donald said.

'*What*?'

I think all the grown-ups said: '*What?*' at once
and looked so stern that poor Donald became scared,
for his voice was wobbling when he said to me: 'It *is*,
Shona! *You* saw it too when the launch came with its
big white light!'—and he blinked up at me through
his glasses.

'Saw what, Donald?'

'Porontium—*x-x-x-x*!' he shouted. 'On the boxes
up there!'

He was pointing up to the wall of the cave above the
entrance, away up above all our heads.

'Dickson,' the detective said, 'steady this boat for
me, will you?'

He took a torch out of his pocket and said: 'Now,
Donald, where did you see these boxes?'

'Up there,' Donald said, pointing. 'Up there, above the door.'

The tall detective climbed up on the highest part of the boat and shone the torch high up on the rock, on the dry part above where the water had been. Then he jumped down.

'Donald is quite right,' he said. 'They *are* up there. Wilson, you and Dickson stay here. Miss Cameron, may I use your telephone?'

'Of course!' Aunt said.

'You and the children had better come back to the house,' he said. 'Those boxes of stuff are not good company,' and he ran away ahead of us along the beach.

'Aunt,' I said, 'it seems as if—'

'Oh, Shona, it's all right. It's just that I'm so flabbergasted I don't know what to say!'

By the time we got back to the house, our own village policeman was already there on his bicycle and the detective inspector was speaking on the telephone.

'Is that Arder Aerodrome? Put me on to your Security Officer, please,' he said and then he told them about the boxes being in the cave. 'You're coming over? Good!'

He put the telephone down, looked at us and said: '*Happy* New Year!'

'Will they come over in the Air Sea Rescue launch, sir?' Neil asked.

'I suppose so.'

'Oh, Aunt, may we go down to the beach? Not round the Point — *our* beach only?'

'Yes, all right. But not round the Point, remember, and don't get in anybody's way.'

We had just reached the edge of the water, for the tide was a long way out now, when we heard the roar of the launch starting up over at the aerodrome and then it came out from the pier and came tearing across the Firth, making huge frothy waves that sparkled in the sun. It stopped out in the deep channel as it had done on Saturday night and put down its little boat and the men rowed in behind the Point to the cave. We did not even want to go round there for it was much better to watch the launch and wave to the men on it and soon we saw the little boat go back. They put the boxes up on to the launch and then came rowing back to *our* beach this time. Three airmen and an officer, they were.

The detective inspector came down from the house, Inspector Wilson and Constable Dickson came round from the cave and they all stood in a circle, talking. We stood back, well out of the way and went on looking at the launch.

'Gosh,' Neil said, 'I *wish* we could get a sail in it!'

'There's no good wishing for an impossible thing like that,' I told him.

'It would be x-x-x-x if we could, though, Shona!' Donald said.

Suddenly the detective inspector shouted : 'Shona, come, here! Come here, the three of you!'

We went over and he said : 'Where is this stone with the squiggles and crosses and numbers on it that you were telling me about?'

'Up at the Old Fort,' I said.

'Is it a clue, sir?' Donald asked.

'"I bit my arm and sucked the blood and cried a clue! a clue!"' Neil said, very dramatic.

'Where is the Old Fort?' Inspector Wilson asked.

'Over the hill there. Not far. We'll show you,' I said.

'All right. Come on!'

We all went tramping off together, up to the house first to tell Aunt where we were going and then on up the path over the hill to the Old Fort.

We had a bit of a laugh at Inspector Wilson and the Air Force officer wriggling through the hole in the wall, because they were both a little too fat for it and the detective inspector was very funny, teasing them.

Inside, they all stood looking down at the stone and the squiggles for a long time, not saying anything and the detective inspector was frowning all over his forehead. The Air Force men stood back a bit, not seeming to be so interested in the squiggles and they began to talk among themselves.

'You'd better stay over here till high water, Jenkins,'

the officer said, 'and get that yacht out of the cave for the police.'

'Yes, sir, It won't be high water till after dark, though, sir.'

'I'll just check it.'

The officer took a little blue book out of his pocket and looked in it. 'Twenty-two twelve hours,' he said. 'You'd better leave it today and come over tomorrow forenoon.'

'Right, sir.'

The detective inspector, who was still staring at the figures and squiggles on the stone, suddenly went: 'Bang!' with the fist of his right hand into the palm of his left.

'I've got it!' he said. 'Look in your book again! Is it high tide at O four twenty-one on the second of January? Tomorrow?'

'Can't be,' the officer said. 'There's a bit over twelve hours between high water and high water.'

'Oh, dash it!' The detective looked disappointed for a moment.

'But O four twenty-one is *low* water tomorrow morning,' the officer said, looking up from his little book.

'So that's it! They've got arrangements for both!' the detective said, pointing down at the stone. 'Look at that!'

And we all looked down at the 1 which was for that

day, the first of January, and at the 22.12 which was for twelve minutes past ten at night and at the 2 which was for the second of January and the 04.21 which was for twenty-one minutes past four in the morning.

'Let's get out of here,' the detective said, 'and carefully, everybody! Try not to move any of these stones. We don't want them to know we have been here!'

He did not make any jokes this time about Inspector Wilson eating too much and being too fat to wriggle through the hole.

When we were outside and a bit away from the Old Fort, we all sat down in the sun on some boulders and the detective took out his notebook where he had made a copy of the drawing that was on the stone.

'This top X is the Old Fort up there,' he said, 'and this next one is the cave and this third one —'

'—is the hangar where the *Jupiter* is!' the Air Force officer said and Jenkins the airman gave a long, low whistle.

'Jenkins,' the detective said, 'you don't have to get that boat out of the cave for us. We'll just leave the *Lady Fair* where she is and wait for these gentlemen to come for her either tonight or early tomorrow morning. What a surprise they'll get when they find that their nice little boxes of candy aren't there any more!' and he picked Donald up, swung him round in a circle, put him down again and said: '*Happy* New Year!'

'Let's go back to the house,' he said next and, then,

to the Air Force officer: 'Can you help us out with
some men from the aerodrome if we need them?'

'As many as you like,' the officer said.

When we arrived back at the house, Aunt put all the
men into the sitting-room because that is where her
telephone is and said to us: 'You three come to the
kitchen with me. We've got a lot to do. All these men
have to be fed.'

As the day went on, the house became fuller and
fuller of policemen who came in three cars which were

shut up and hidden away in Aunt's old barn and, although the Air Force officer went away, he left Jenkins and another airman and their little boat. The policemen were not wearing their uniforms but had ordinary clothes and when we looked in through the sitting-room window once, during the afternoon, the detective inspector had them all round the table where Donald's map was spread out and he was drawing little rings all over it with a red pencil (see map).

When it began to get dark, all the policemen went out and went away up the hill behind the house and then Aunt allowed us to go into the sitting-room, where the map was still spread out on the table and the detective inspector, Inspector Wilson and the two airmen were standing round it. It had a lot of rings of blue pencil on it now too (see map).

'What are all the coloured rings for, sir?' Neil asked.

'The blue ones are where the policemen are going now,' the detective inspector said. 'You see, if these men come for the boat tonight at high tide at 10.12, they'll have to come by water because they can't get to the cave any other way. I've got an idea they'll come down from the north by car to the Old Fort, bringing a canoe or a dinghy with them, carry it down to the sea and float quietly towards the cave with the tide. That is, if they come at 10.12 tonight. If they come at low water at 4.21 tomorrow morning, they'll be able to walk round to the cave from this side or the other side, so the red rings are the points where the policemen will be watching from then. We've got to get them absolutely red-handed at the cave, you see, so that they can't bluff their way out by telling us that they were just fishing or something — We've made a fine mess of your map, Donald, but I'll get you a new one.'

'No, thank you, sir,' Donald said. 'I'd like to have that one back when you've finished with it because it's a real live clue.'

At eight o' clock, the detective inspector and the two airmen put on their overcoats and went out and then Inspector Wilson said : 'Well, I'd better get out to the barn.'

'What are you going to do in the barn, sir?' Neil asked.

'I'm radio control, lad,' he said. 'The policemen have got walkie-talkies and they'll be in touch with me in one of the cars in the barn. So will the Air Force on the other side of the Firth.'

'Oh, sir —' Neil started to say.

'No, Neil,' Aunt said. 'You'd only be in the way.'

'Oh, well, if he kept quiet —' Inspector Wilson said.

'Inspector, if Neil goes they'll *all* have to go, so NO,' Aunt said very firmly.

'Well, why not?' Inspector Wilson said. 'You come too, Miss Cameron, and keep them in order. You can sit in one of the cars and hear everything that goes on.'

'Oh, *Aunt*—' we said, but there was not any need to persuade her. I felt that she was as keen to go to the barn as we were.

We all got our coats and followed Inspector Wilson outside, walking very, very softly and not speaking. It was terribly quiet and absolutely pitch dark, for it would be three days before the new moon would come up, according to my diary.

As we tiptoed round to the barn in the black silence, I was almost afraid to breathe in case the criminals were lurking somewhere about and would hear me.

7. *The Capture in the Cave*

Inside the barn, the four of us huddled into the front seat of one of the cars by the light of Inspector Wilson's torch, Donald on Aunt's knee, me in the middle and Neil at the steering-wheel. Inspector Wilson put on the dashboard light and the car clock with its luminous dial was right in front of me. It was exactly five past eight. Inspector Wilson switched on the radio but nothing came out of it except a faint humming noise that made you know it was switched on. Then he went away and got into another car just alongside of us. It was all quite sort of scary, being so quiet, and the dashboard lights made all the faces look sort of green in colour.

Suddenly, a voice said: 'Testing!' quite quietly, but I nearly jumped out of my skin until I saw Inspector Wilson's green face smiling at us from the next car and realised it was he who had spoken.

After that, the men who were out at the places that had blue rings on the map started answering: 'A— Apple, B—Bertie,' and so on and then we heard: 'Yard,' and realised it was the detective inspector's voice. I thought it was short for 'Scotland Yard' but we found out afterwards that his name was 'Yarde'. Then, after him, we heard: 'R.A.F. One' and 'R.A.F. Two'; Inspector Wilson said: 'Okay, all,' and then everything was all absolutely quiet in the greenish light except for that tiny humming noise from the radio.

Neil and Donald and I usually talk quite a lot and eat sweets any time they are available but, although I had the jar of sweets in my lap that Aunt had given me to bring out, I never even thought of opening it and I did not feel like talking, either. We simply sat there in that greenish light, almost afraid to breathe and listened and listened.

After a very long time, a voice came very low but you could hear the excitement in it all the same.

'C — Charlie, C — Charlie —'

'Come in, Charlie,' Inspector Wilson said, very quickly and quietly.

'Car without lights, canoe on roof, passing south now — over.'

After that, the voices came pouring out of the radio, all low, husky and excited.

'D — David, D — David — car leaving road, heading for Old Fort — over.'

'E — Edward, E — Edward, car stopped — two men — one entering fort — one preparing unload canoe — over.'

There was a pause. I could not breathe.

'E — Edward, E — Edward — canoe unloaded — over.'

'F — Freddie, F — Freddie — canoe launched —

headed down coast — men lying down out of sight —
over.'

There was a pause again and I managed to take a
good deep breath before I heard : 'G — George, G —
George — floating down nicely — over.'

There was a longish pause which was nearly un-
bearable and then Inspector Wilson's voice came :
' Calling H — Harry, H — Harry — '

'H — Harry, H — Harry,' the voice answered.
'Very dark. Very high here. Can hardly see water —
Oh, *BLAST*!'

Out of the radio came a crash, a loud squealing
noise, a hard crackling and then there was a silence that
was suddenly broken by a voice saying : 'Yarde here,
Yarde — Collins is over the cliff in the drink — can
he swim? — Over — '

'Collins is County Police champion swimmer,'
Inspector Wilson's voice said.

'J — Jack, J — Jack!' another voice came shouting

through the radio. 'Canoe passing here—two men paddling like blazes!'

Aunt and Donald and I were all hanging on to one another now and Neil was clinging to the steering-wheel so hard that you could see his knuckles nearly bursting through his skin and suddenly we heard the detective inspector's voice say quite calmly, not dramatically at all: 'Good evening. Looking for your boxes? I'm afraid *we've* got them.' But somehow it felt tremendously dramatic.

Suddenly there were a lot of bangs, a scuffling noise, the noise of men struggling, then more banging and then a big splash before the voice came again: 'Got him, Jenkins? Good. It's against the law to drown *human* rats—Calling control—'

'Control—' Inspector Wilson said.

'Call out the Air Sea Rescue for Collins! Call the other men in. We're just coming round. Over.'

'Oh, goodness!' Aunt said. 'I'm pins and needles all *over*!' and she opened the car door. 'Jump out, Donald.'

When we were out of the car and Neil was saying: 'Gosh! Oh, *gosh*!' over and over again and Donald was jumping up and down and saying: 'X-X-X-X!' Aunt said: 'We might as well make a night of it. Let's go up to the top of the Point and watch them finding Constable Collins. Dear me, he must be cold!'

Up there, it was simply splendid. We ran all the

way, Aunt in front with the torch, because it was so dark that you could not even see the path, but we got to the top in time to see the launches — all *three* of them had come out — streaking across the Firth, then slowing down and playing their search-lights on the water and in no time at all they found Constable Collins and pulled him on board. As soon as he was safe, their engines roared up again and they went streaking back across to the aerodrome until their lights were mixed up with all the other lights and we could not see them any more.

'Gosh, I wish I was Constable Collins!' Neil said. 'I wish *I* could get a sail in the Air Sea Rescue launch!'

'*You* are going to bed!' Aunt said. 'That's where all three of you are going.'

But we did not go to bed right away after all, for when we reached the house the detective inspector asked Aunt to bring us out to the barn. All the policemen were in there, except Constable Collins, of course, and there were two men, one with his clothes soaking wet, handcuffed to two of the policemen.

'Shona, Neil, Donald,' the detective inspector said to us, 'have you ever seen either of these men before?'

The car headlights were shining on them so that their faces looked very white and frightened, but I was sure I had never seen either of them before.

'No,' I said.

'Not me either, sir,' Neil said.

'Not me,' Donald said, staring solemnly through his glasses and shaking his head.

'Not on the train?' Inspector Wilson asked.

'No!' we all said at once.

'All right, men,' the detective inspector said, 'pile in and get off back to Rioch. We'll be along shortly.'

The detective inspector, Inspector Wilson, Constable Dickson, Aunt and the three of us went into the house.

Aunt went to the kitchen to make coffee. Aunt is always making tea and coffee and feeding people but she forgot to tell us to go to bed so we stayed in the sitting-room.

'We haven't got them all rounded up yet, dash it!' Inspector Yarde said. 'Those two we got tonight are the experts who were going to do the job on the Jupiter all right, but my information was that there were seven altogether. Those two we got over at the aerodrome last week with the plans of the hangars on them were only side-kicks, but we had them pulled in *before* the *Lady Fair* came into the Firth here. Now the *Lady Fair* was stolen from Port Sinclair'—he went to the map on the table—'about fifty miles up the coast. I bet these two gentlemen we caught tonight don't bother to do the little dirty jobs, like stealing boats and putting them in caves. It's the small-time ones who have to take these sort of risks for very little pay. No. That information I had has been accurate so far and it definitely said that there were seven in the gang altogether. That means that three more of them are still kicking about.'

'I bet it's those three porters what knocked me *down*!' Donald said.

The detective inspector looked down at him. 'I wouldn't be at all surprised, Donald,' he said, and looked at Inspector Wilson. 'Those three on the train are just the sort of shabby little crooks I mean — the kind that will steal any little thing that's lying about anywhere — even little girls' watches! And they're stupid, those small-time chaps, as a rule. They do silly things, like selling Shona's watch with those initials on it. It annoys me to have caught the two king pins and have let the other three slip through our fingers.'

'You'll catch them yet, sir!' Neil said. 'If we see them again, we'll —'

'If you see them again,' he said, laughing at us, 'dial "O" on the nearest telephone, shout "Rioch Police" and just say "Camerons here" and you'll get either Inspector Wilson or Constable Dickson or me right away!'

'What are you three doing here?' Aunt's voice asked and there she was in the doorway with the tray of coffee and sandwiches. 'Haven't you had enough for one day? Brush your teeth and get off to bed. There's not time for baths tonight. Good night.'

We said good night and went upstairs but we took a long time to go to bed because Neil had become very dramatic now with all the excitement and he infected Donald and me with it, for being dramatic is something like measles. People can catch it from one another.

'Rioch Police! Camerons here!' Neil kept shouting.

'X-X-X-X!' Donald kept shouting.

'Rioch Police! Camerons here!'

We did not even hear the last police car drive away and we were doing: 'C—Charlie, C—Charlie, car without lights, canoe on roof, passing south now, over—' when Aunt appeared in the bathroom.

'Over!' she said. 'Who wants to go over my knee and get a good smacking? Tomorrow's the last day of your holidays and you won't be fit for a thing!' so that was the end of being dramatic for that night.

When I got into bed, I felt like a balloon when the air has gone out of it, all limp and droopy. It had been such a splendid holidays that nothing could ever be as splendid again. We slept late the next morning and we had just finished breakfast and were helping Aunt to light the sitting-room fire when her telephone rang.

'Oh, dash it!' she said and took off her fire-cleaning gloves.

'Miss Cameron here. Oh, yes? Yes. Good morning, Squadron-Leader. Oh, that's very kind of you— they'd simply love it. Yes. Yes, I can drive round the end of the Firth. What time? Any time that suits *you,* Squadron-Leader. Two o'clock? All right, we'll be there at two o'clock and thank you. Goodbye.'

'Guess what?' she said to us. 'It's something for you three.'

'Sweets?' Neil asked.

'No.'

'A present of some kind?' I asked.

'Yes. Sort of. More of a treat.'

'What's a Squaddin' Leader?' Donald asked.

'It was the aerodrome!' Neil said. 'We've been invited to see the aerodrome!'

'Even better than that.'

'It *can't* be better'n *that*!' Neil said.

'You've been invited to the aerodrome to see the Jupiter—'

'The *Jupiter*?'

'—and go for a sail in one of the Air Sea Rescue launches on her practice run this afternoon!'

'Oh, golly, googly, gosh and golly!'

'X-X-X-X!'

'Aunt,' I said, 'could you press my tartan trousers now I've got them back? I can't go sailing in the launch in this silly skirt!'

It was all absolutely tremendous. I cannot describe the Jupiter properly, because I did not know that aeroplanes were so enormous when you are close to them, and, when we went into the hangar, I was looking around behind a big black thing in front of me for the Jupiter before I discovered that the big black thing was its nose wheel and that I was standing under its nose. I had a very narrow squeak, because I was just going to ask Neil where the Jupiter was and I was so glad afterwards that I kept quiet.

I liked the sail in the Air Sea Rescue launch best of all, although tea was very good too. We had it in a big hall called the 'Officers' Mess', but it was not in the least a messy place, so I asked Aunt about this name on the way home and it seems that 'mess', used in that way, means something to do with food, like in 'mess of pottage' in the Bible.

After tea, we got into the Squadron-Leader's car and he drove us down to the other end of the aerodrome to the shore of the Firth and there was a little harbour with the three launches and several other smaller boats. Right across the water we could see the Point and Aunt's house and the Old Fort and our beach and everything, but at this side of the Firth there was no beach, only deep water right up to the pier.

We went on board and down a little ladder to a place behind a glass screen, like the windscreen of a car only bigger, but it was too high for us to see out through, so some airmen brought boxes for us to stand on. Then, off we went, slowly at first, with the engines just going chug-chug-chug as we went backwards out of the harbour, but then the launch pointed its nose down the Firth, there was that thrilling roar and we seemed to jump from one wave to the next as if we were on horseback. If it had not been for the Squadron-

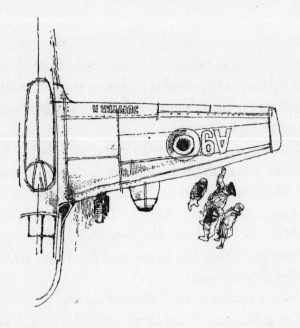

Leader and an airman holding us from behind, we would have fallen off our boxes.

I wished we could go on and on for ever but, of course, things never last for ever and soon we turned round in a big circle and started roaring back up the Firth. When we were in sight of the harbour again, the Squadron-Leader said to the man at the wheel: 'Check her back now,' and then explained to us that they had to test the boat at all her speeds and not just at her fastest. When she was throttled right down so that she was hardly moving at all, he took us up to the front part of the deck where the roundel is painted so that the aeroplanes can see it from above and showed us the big searchlight, while the airman behind the screen down below made it swivel about. I was sorry it was not night-time so that we could have it on and light up the water, but if it had been dark we could not have seen the coast-line swooshing past when we were sailing at high speed.

Neil was so overcome with everything that he hardly spoke at all on the way home, which was so unusual that when we reached the house and had put the car in the barn, Aunt said:'Are you feeling seasick, Neil?'

'*Me*?' he burst out. 'No! Seasick! NO! When I'm old enough, I'm going to join the Air Force and be an Air Sea Rescue man!'

'Not a Jupiter pilot?' Donald asked.

'Or a Scotland Yard detective?' I asked. 'You've got the right hair for it.'

'The Squadron-Leader had red hair too!' Neil said. 'All the best people have red hair!'

'And *none* of the best people have swelled heads!' Aunt said.

We had to go to bed early that night, to be ready for our journey the next day, but we did not mind. It had been such a wonderful holidays.

8. Camerons on the Train!

Aunt drove us to Rioch station the next morning. When she telephoned to Father after we arrived, she told him, of course, about how I had lost my watch and how we had got into the siding and everything and Father asked to speak to me and gave me quite a ticking-off over the telephone. Then he spoke to Neil, and *he* got a ticking-off too and Father ended up by saying that we were evidently too silly to travel alone after all and he had better come up with the car and fetch us back. It made Neil and me feel pretty small for a while but Aunt did a splendid thing. She rang him up and told him how we had helped the police that day at Rioch after *Pirates' Gold* and she did *not* tell him about us going round the Point and getting marooned in the cave, so Father gave in and said we could travel back to Inverdaviot by ourselves.

'Now, listen,' Aunt said when we were in the compartment, '*don't* go prowling about the corridor staring at people and, if you go to the lavatory, don't take off your watch, Shona!'

'I can't,' I said, 'because the police still have it.'

'That's a blessing anyway. Now, another thing. This train stops at Moorland Junction for about quarter of an hour to pick up people off the train from the north. You will sit still and not leave the compartment. Promise?'

We promised.

'We didn't stop at Moorland Junction coming up,' Neil said. 'It's only about ten miles out of Rioch, isn't it?'

'Yes, but a goods train got derailed here in the station early this morning so they're bringing the north train in to Moorland Junction instead of in here.'

'Where's it derailed? Will we see it?' Neil asked.

'You probably will, as you go past. I saw the crane up ahead there.'

'Oh, gosh!'

'X-X-X-X!'

The train gave a jerk and started to puff-puff-puff out of the station and we waved to Aunt through the window and then began to watch for the derailed goods train, but there was only a coal truck lying on its side and a heap of coal all over the rails next to ours. The crane was quite big, but not as big as the ones in a quarry that Father took us to see once, so, after we had seen it, I climbed up and put the boys' cowboy hats in the rack, but they kept their holster belts with their water pistols on.

In odd moments, during the holidays, Neil and Donald had been practising drawing both pistols at the same time and Neil was quite good at it now. Neil seems just naturally to be quite good at anything that is dramatic, but Donald is not really the dramatic type so, when they started practising the double-draw again now, and Donald's pistols had fallen on the floor and under the seats a few times, he got tired of it very soon and sat down to read his newspaper.

'*Dram*atic arrest on lonely north-east coast!' he read out. 'Sa*bot*eurs overpowered in cave!'

Neil and I gathered round him and began to read too.

'Only last night did the police reveal that two further arrests had been made in the sabotage case in which two arrests were made at Arder Aerodrome ten days ago. The police are now confident that the entire gang are rounded up.'

The newspaper then went on to tell all over again, as newspapers often do, about the two men arrested at the aerodrome.

'But what about the men what knocked me *down*?' Donald said. 'They were going to catch them too!'

'I tell you what!' Neil said, going all dramatic. 'That's a blind! Mr. Yarde is just pretending he is not looking for these three men any more. It's a blind!'

'Oh, you and your blinds!' I said, for I was quite determined not to let Neil get dramatic on this journey, for it only leads us into trouble in the end. Once we were home, I thought, he could be as dramatic as he pleased, but not till we were out of this train.

'When Mr. Yarde and I were discussing the case,'

he started off in his grandest voice and was just about to make up a real fairy-tale, when the train put its brakes on and we came into Moorland Junction.

It is not much of a junction, only two platforms and the branch line going away through the valley, but we watched two truck-loads of sheep being unloaded and it was very interesting to see the sheep-dogs looking after them and seeing that they did not jump off the platform on to the rails or anything.

'Ten more minutes yet,' Neil said, looking at his watch when the sheep had been driven away.

'If the train from the north is in,' I said. 'Aunt said it is late sometimes.'

'What d'you think that is over there that the sheep came out of?' Neil asked. 'A balloon?'

'Neil Cameron, stop being uppish and cheeky!'

'Well, that's the north —'

'*There* they are!' Donald said.

'Who?'

'The men what knocked me *down*!'

We looked where he was pointing and, sure enough, there were three small, thin men, one with his hat pulled down over his ears, one with a scarf all muffled up round his mouth as if he had toothache and the third one scuttling along as if he were very frightened. They started to come towards our carriage, so we three jumped into a heap in one corner and got behind Donald's newspaper. The little window at the top was

open and, as they went past, we heard one of them say :
' Nod much peoples on dees train.'

' It's *them* ! ' Neil whispered and then we heard the
door of the next compartment slam shut.

' We've still got five minutes ! ' Neil said. ' There's
a 'phone box right there on the platform ! '

' But, Neil, we promised Aunt—'

' There's always exceptions ! ' Neil said.

This is what Aunt had said when she told us that
she did not tell Father about us going and getting ourselves marooned.

' I'm going to 'phone ! ' he said.

' Then we're *all* going ! ' I said. ' Come on, Donald ! '

We ran up the corridor away from the compartment
where the men were, jumped out on to the platform
and flung ourselves into the telephone box.

' Here goes ! ' Neil said and lifted the receiver and
dialled ' O '.

' Rioch Police ! ' he shouted and then : ' Camerons
here ! '

' Bend *down*,' I said, ' so that Donald can hear ! '

We all heard quite clearly the detective inspector's
voice say : ' Yarde here ! Where are you ? '

' Moorland Junction and—'

' —the men what knocked me *down* is on the
train ! ' Donald shouted.

' Honest ? You're sure ? '

' Absolutely spifflicating certain, sir ! ' Neil said.

'Don't let them see you but get back on the train! See you soon!' the voice said and there was a click and the line went dead.

We went back inside the train further up and walked down through the luggage van to our compartment and then we all climbed right up on to a corner seat facing the corridor and spread out the newsaper in front of us. It was Neil who had the idea of poking little holes in the paper so that we could see anybody passing.

Along the coast here, all the way from Moorland Junction almost to Inverdaviot, the road and the railway run side by side, crossing and re-crossing one another and, just outside behind us, on the side of the train opposite to the corridor, was the road with the cars flying along.

'Shona, you watch the road for the police car. I'll watch the corridor,' Neil said.

The train should have left about five minutes ago, I saw from Neil's watch.

'Maybe Mr. Yarde 'phoned telling them to hold it,' Neil said, but, just then, the train blew its whistle and started to move and, in the very same moment, I saw the police car on the road down below, just about to turn into the station yard.

'Oh, Neil, they've missed it!' I said.

'Never mind. They'll come on.'

And they did. I could see Mr. Yarde's red hair quite clearly, sitting beside the policeman who was driving and there were two more policemen in the back.

After Moorland Junction, the road and railway go over miles and miles of moors with no houses or anything except the aerodrome inside its big, high wire fence (see map). We usually look forward to seeing the aerodrome, but we did not look at it today at all. Neil and Donald looked through the holes in the paper at the corridor and I watched the police car coming along the road beside us down below.

All of a sudden, I felt Neil going stiff and heard Donald whispering: 'That's them!' and the men went past our compartment, so we crept along the seat and peeped out of the corner of the window. They seemed to be arguing and pointing out towards the road and one of them was making a lot of gestures around the door of the train. They had seen the police car!

Along this part of the line, especially in winter, the train goes very slowly because the moorland is swampy and gets flooded quite often. I suddenly knew what the men were going to do.

'They're going to jump off in the swampy bit!' I said to Neil. 'They'll get away among all that heather and those bushes and trees!'

'Oh, dash it!' Neil said, very like Mr. Yarde.

'Neil, I'm going to pull it!'

'Pull what?'

'The communication cord, fathead!'

'But, *Shona*,' Donald whispered, 'it's pen*alt*y five pounds!'

'I don't care!' I said, for the train was going more and more slowly.

With my fingers crossed in my mind and my heart beating very fast, I jumped on the seat, took hold of the cord and pulled down hard. The train put its brakes on at once and then everything happened so fast I can hardly tell about it.

'They're going to jump!' Neil shouted and, sliding the door of our compartment open with a bang, he sprang out into the corridor with Donald behind him.

'You *can't* get away!' he shouted, being very dramatic. 'There's Camerons on the train!'

Then both he and Donald did the double-draw and neither of Donald's pistols fell this time and there was an absolute shower of black stuff that went all over the men's faces and into their eyes and up their noses and they began to cough and splutter.

'Dese demn keeds!' one of them said, sneezing, and

then the guard came running up the corridor and Mr. Yarde and the policemen came scrambling up the embankment.

'What's all this?' the guard said, looking at the three men all dripping with the black, sticky stuff.

'It's Draper's Dependable Dye, sir,' Neil said, putting his pistols back into their holsters, but one of Donald's fell on the floor this time and I had to put it away for him.

We did not have to do any more explaining to the guard, though, because Mr. Yarde attended to everything for us and the policemen took the three men away down to the car.

'You can start your train again now, Guard,' Mr. Yarde said, 'and how much is the fare to Inverdaviot? I'm going to see these three safely home.'

'That's all right, sir,' the guard said. 'You're welcome.' And then he looked at Neil and Donald. 'What did you say was in these pistols of yours?' he asked.

'Draper's Dependable Dye, sir,' Neil told him.

'I must try it sometime when I meet somebody I don't like,' he said and went away, and all the other people who had gathered round went back to their compartments.

It was great fun having Mr. Yarde with us the rest of the way to Inverdaviot for, as he said, he was only joking with the guard when he said he was going to see us safely home.

'Will we have to pay pen*alt*y five pounds?' Donald asked him.

'Of course not! You don't pay a pen*alt*y for catching criminals.'

'No. And they knocked me *down*!' Donald said.

The train was only half an hour late in getting to Inverdaviot after all and when Father saw us in the compartment, he walked along the platform beside us until the train stopped.

'Ssh!' Neil said. 'Pretend you don't know us, sir!'

Mr. Yarde sat still, not speaking, while Father helped us down.

'Well, you didn't get into trouble this time, did you?' Father asked as Mr. Yarde got out of the train.

'Father,' Neil said, 'this is Detective Inspector Yarde from *Scotland* Yard and we got into so *much* trouble that he had to bring us home!'

Father stared at Mr. Yarde and then back at us, frowning.

'Oh, Neil!' I said. 'Father, it was like this——'

'There were three crooks on the train, very small-time stuff——' Neil said grandly, being very dramatic.

'And they knocked me *down*!' Donald said, looking up very gravely at Father through his glasses.

'Be quiet, the lot of you!' Father said. 'Detective Inspector — you *are* a detective inspector?'

'Yes, Yarde's my name. It was like this, Mr. Cameron—'

Mr. Yarde came home with us and had a meal, which was splendid because it meant that Iain, our little brother, knows him too now and was not left out and then he—Mr. Yarde, I mean, not Iain—went back to Rioch on the evening train.

We talked and talked about everything for days, answering all Father and Mother's questions and we accidentally let out that we had been marooned in the cave, but Father did not scold us. All he said was: 'I bet poor Aunt was glad to put you on the train for home!'

It was about eight weeks later—at mid-term— that we got the letter from Birmingham one morning addressed to Neil, Donald and me with all our names on the envelope and when we opened it, it was from the managing director of the chemical firm whose lorry with the Porontium 106 was stolen. Inside it were three cheques, one for each of us and each one for twenty whole pounds. Imagine it, when we thought we might have to pay pen*alt*y five pounds, as Donald calls it! There was also a very nice letter, thanking us for what we had done to help the police and it ended: 'I am very thankful that Draper's Dependable Dye, which is one of the many products of this company, and Camerons were on the train.'

I think Mr. Yarde must have told him about Neil

going all dramatic and saying : ' There's Camerons on the train ! ' but, anyhow, that is why I have called this story of our last Christmas holidays ' Camerons on the Train '.

THE END